MILES LEDOUX

OVERKILL

Winter in Veil, Book 7

First published by ABCs 2025

First edition

ISBN: 978-1-882508-87-7

Cover art by Rachel Kelli
Editing by Julie Mianecki

This book was professionally typeset on Reedsy.
Find out more at reedsy.com

Prologue

In the distance, a shot rang out.

Deputy Benno sat up in bed. "Great Scott!" he exclaimed. He threw aside the covers, leaped out of his four-poster bed, hastily tugged on a dressing gown, and flew out the door.

A silver moon shone through ten-foot-high windows, filling the hallway with eerie light. Leafless branches shook in the turbulent wind, tapping frenetically against the panes. Benno was filled with trepidation as he hastened down the corridor.

He saw a crowd gathered at an open door at the end of the hall. "What's happened?" he demanded.

A petite, beautiful young woman in a negligée pivoted toward him dramatically and regarded him with wide amber eyes. In a husky whisper, Violet proclaimed, *"Murder!"*

Benno put a hand to his chest, threw back his head, and gasped. Thunder and lightning boomed.

I

Violet woke up with a start. Something was tapping on her window from outside. Sitting up and squinting through the swirling ice and snow, she could just make out a branch whipping against the glass. Grunting, she lay down again to go back to sleep.

Then she sat up straight. In the two months she'd lived in this house, there had never been a branch this close to her window. Once again peering outside, she examined the branch as closely as she could. The false dawn was just bright enough to reveal the ice coating the bough. Momentarily, the wind died down, letting the snow slow its dance long enough for Violet to see that the entire tree, in fact, was coated in a thick layer of ice, and the added weight was causing it to lean over dramatically—bringing its branches closer to her window.

This was no ordinary December storm. This was an *ice* storm.

Violet twisted in place to check the time. The face of her digital clock was blank. Reaching over, she pressed the switch on her bedside lamp. Nothing happened.

A minute later, pulling on her bathrobe, Violet stepped into the hall. She shivered, hugging herself. The lights were off in the bathroom next to her room, but someone had set an electric lantern on the counter.

I

From the other end of the hall approached a walking wooly blanket with eyeballs. The top of it wriggled, and out popped the head of a teenage girl.

"Power outage?" asked Violet.

"Yup," said Cy through chattering teeth. She gathered Violet into the blanket and they went downstairs.

Cy's mother, Jen, was already in the kitchen. She was fully dressed, but she seemed more adapted to the cold than her daughter, as the only winter garb she wore was a wool cap, her dirty blond hair spilling out from beneath it. With a long match, she ignited one of the burners on the gas stove and cooked a breakfast of scrambled eggs.

"We have a generator, right, Mom?" asked Cy.

"Yes, we do," Jen said emphatically as she scraped egg onto Violet's dish. "I made sure of that when we moved in. After we eat, I'll get it hooked up."

"Do you need help with that?" Violet offered.

Jen shook her head, taking a swig of black coffee and sitting down next to them at the long rectangular table set against the kitchen wall.

For a moment, the three of them ate in comfortable silence, light and warmth emanating from the nearby kerosene heater. A calico cat hopped onto the bench next to Cy and curled up against her, purring.

"I was having a weird dream just before I woke up," Violet remarked.

"What was it about?" asked Cy, though her attention was mostly on the cat she was petting. Jen, likewise, seemed mesmerized by the ice storm cavorting beyond the window.

Violet shrugged. "I don't remember."

Several moments passed.

Then, one at a time, Cy and her mother ceased what they were doing and turned to stare at her.

"Say that again?" said Cy.

"I said I don't—" All at once Violet set down her fork and stared back at them wonderingly. "I don't remember! I don't remember what I dreamed!" A moment later she added, "Come to think of it, I don't think I remember *any* of my dreams." For Violet this was a rare occurrence. From the moment she'd woken up in Veil two months ago, Violet could perfectly remember everything she saw and did. Now it seemed there might actually be a large number of gaps in that memory. She wasn't sure whether to feel concerned or relieved.

"What does that mean?" asked Cy, echoing Violet's thoughts.

Violet had no idea, and was about to say so when all three of them were startled by a knock at the front door. Jen stood to answer it but paused when her cell phone rang.

"I'll get it, Mom," Cy volunteered, heading for the door as Jen answered her phone.

A tall, broad-shouldered silhouette occupied the front porch. Dawn was approaching, but true morning light was still a ways off. Leaning through the doorway, Cy squinted at the face under the hood. "Fran?"

Fran Dosley, who lived next door, pulled her hood back once Cy had invited her inside. She brushed snow from her face and her short, graying hair.

"Did you guys lose power, too?" asked Cy.

"Everyone's out of power," Fran replied shortly. "Said so on the radio."

"Oh my god. Are you guys okay?"

"No." Fran tended to be terse and blunt. "The radio's the only thing that's working, and we can't get our kerosene heaters on."

"We've got a couple extras. We don't need to heat the whole house."

"What we need is hot water."

"Well, we've got a gas stove, so we can heat some..." A blast of chilly air blew open the door, which they'd left ajar. Tugging it shut, Cy amended, "On second thought, why don't you all just come over here?"

Fran hesitated. "Would that be all right with your mother?"

Jen, just then passing by while still on the phone, threw a "Yes!" over her shoulder.

Fran pulled her hood back up. "Be right back."

Cy and Violet managed to clean up the living room just before Fran returned with the rest of her family in tow. One of them was a very short woman—even shorter than Violet—who had evidently trudged through snow piled as high as her waist. The other was a tired-looking teenage girl with white-blond hair, carrying a boxy object covered with two blankets. As she set it on the coffee table, it emitted a cooing sound, giving away that it contained the fourth and smallest member of the family.

"Oh, shoot, I forgot Rosie's formula," lamented the teen girl.

Fran put out a hand as the girl moved toward the door. "No, Kristy, I'll go back and get it. You stay inside." Not waiting for a response, she headed out into the storm.

"Thanks," Kristy mumbled.

"There's some water heating on the stove," Cy told the newcomers, "but Mom's about to get the generator started, so soon you'll have all you need."

"Oh, thank you, honey," wheezed the short woman, catching her breath. Like Fran, she'd carried several parcels from next door, which she'd set down in the corner of the room.

"Can we make you guys some breakfast?" offered Violet.

Kristy abruptly pivoted, not having seen Violet till just then. "Oh, hi!" she said with a sudden bright smile.

Glancing uncertainly at Cy, Violet returned the smile. "Hello."

It seemed to take Kristy a moment to remember Violet's question. "Oh, no thank you."

"You sure?"

"I started applying for colleges, like you said!"

Though taken aback, Violet remembered the conversation from a few weeks ago, when the Dosleys had her and the Grogans over for dinner. "Oh, good," she said encouragingly.

"Do you think I could use you as a reference?"

"Oh. Um..." Violet wouldn't have minded, but she doubted she would make a very good reference when even she had no idea about her true identity. Rosie saved her the trouble of pointing this out when the baby started to cry. Kristy took her out of the carrier and started to nurse her just as Jen returned, putting her phone away.

"I have to report to the station right now," she announced. "Joy, do you think you could get the generator going if I show you where it is?"

Joy hesitated. "Well, me, no, but Fran probably could."

"Okay, good. I'll show her before I leave. You two," she said, pointing at Cy and Violet, "the sheriff's looking for volunteers to help at the emergency shelters around town. Do you want in?"

"Sure," Violet said immediately.

Cy raised her hand, as if she were in class. "Helping how?"

"Probably setting up cots, preparing food, making sure everyone has enough blankets, that sort of thing."

"Oh, yeah, I can do that."

"Then get your coats on. We leave in five minutes."

* * *

Violet expected that Jen would have to take it slow as she drove them into town to the sheriff's station, and she was right—but it wasn't just due to the icy road conditions, as she'd thought. The freezing rain was beginning to abate; as the air cleared, it made visible the devastation left in the storm's wake. Every tree in sight was practically bent double, weighed down by a thick icy coating on all the branches, some of which had broken off. Avoiding these obstacles was what necessitated Jen's cautious driving. Just into town, they discovered most of the roads hadn't yet been plowed. They had to park on the outskirts and walk the rest of the way, holding each other up so they didn't slip and fall.

Trees weren't the only things sagging under the extra weight of the ice. Telephone wires hovered mere feet from the ground, utility poles on the verge of teetering over. If this happened, the few cars that had apparently been left parked on the street overnight were in danger of being crushed. There was little that could be done about this: the cars themselves were encased in shells of ice, inches thick. At least one car they passed had already had its roof caved in by a fallen branch. Another tree had cracked at its base and collapsed against a house, gouging a hole in the wall. Repair crews swarmed throughout the village, doing whatever they could to alleviate the damage.

The inside of the sheriff's station was more crowded than Violet had ever seen it, crammed as it was with deputies and volunteers like her and Cy. The tall, bearded, barrel-chested Sheriff Dubowski waved for attention at the front of the room. As everyone quieted down, he rumbled, "Listen up! We are in a state of emergency! I'm glad to see how many volunteers have turned up to help—we badly need it.

"Just so you know, the Veil Fire Department has taken point on this whole situation. We of this department have to do our jobs *and* assist them. *They* are in charge, we are their backup. Is that clear?"

A broken chorus of "Yes, sir"s answered him.

"One of our top priorities is to clear the roads of debris so the snowplows can do their job. Deputy Trent, I want you to take three volunteers and go assist with that on Main Street. Powell, I want you to do the same thing near the hospital. If you see anyone stuck in their driveway, help them out if you can."

"Ziegler, you're familiar with the farms outside Veil. I want you and two volunteers to orbit the town, go from farm to farm, see if anyone needs help with animals trapped by storm wreckage. If they need supplies or transportation, call it in.

"Which brings me to you two, Tan and Hayden. We have two ATVs at our disposal. Tan, you're responsible for transporting people: doctors to patients, repairmen to wherever they're most needed, etcetera. Hayden, you'll be delivering supplies, especially..." He consulted a nearby computer screen. "Food to road workers, firewood slash kerosene slash batteries to people still at home who don't have power, and..." He squinted. "Flashlights and—*calculators?* What? Oh, to the grocery store. Jesus." With a quick sigh he went on, "We've opened two emergency shelters, one at the Presbyterian Church and one in a karate studio—the one in the old UPS storage building—but we're gonna need to open more. Deputy Grogan, I want you to take four volunteers and help turn the community center into a shelter. There's another one that just started taking people in, on Mountain Circle, but they're severely understaffed." He did a quick scan to see which deputies were left. "Derrick, Benno, and, uh...Violet, head over there, do what you can to help."

I

Several pairs of eyes seemed to zero in on Violet when the sheriff mentioned her name, which made her rather wish he hadn't. A few of them also murmured at the mention of Deputy Benno, the rookie deputy who had made headlines last month by taking down a serial killer who had been menacing the town.

Once the sheriff dismissed everyone, Violet sidled through the crowd toward Deputy Benno.

"Sheriff," Benno asked just then, "What's the address for the shelter on Mountain Circle?"

"Number thirteen."

Violet stopped in her tracks. *Wait,* she thought. *I know that address.* After a moment, she closed her eyes and deflated. *Oh no.*

II

"As the mayor of Veil, opening up my home to people in need is the least I can do."

Mayor Elijah Pressler was glad he'd remembered to silence his phone. It sat by his elbow, just on the edge of his peripheral vision. The screen lit up every time he received a new notification; a quick glance told him they were all texts from his assistant, Brenda. He held back a sigh of irritation. He'd told her not to disturb him during this interview.

"How many people are currently using your home as a shelter?" asked the basso profundo voice issuing from the speaker by his computer.

"About thirty, thirty-five," Pressler replied, knowing it was closer to twenty-five.

"And how many more could you take in?"

"Oh, about fifteen or twenty," Pressler told the webcam, "although I'm informed that the community center will soon open as a new shelter, and that might be more convenient for most people to go to, as it's in the center of town."

"Thank you, Mr. Mayor. We know you're busy. We'll reach out again later."

"Thanks, Rod." Pressler switched off the webcam. When he

was sure the live feed was cut, he sagged in his chair. "Goddamn winter," he muttered.

Not in the mood to read all of Brenda's texts, he decided to go find the woman and let her harangue him in person. Locating her wasn't difficult, as she was just outside his study door when he opened it. She wore glasses with a strap, and had a long, gray ponytail.

"Sir, we have a problem—well, ten problems—"

Hastily, Pressler yanked the woman into the room, shut the door, and put a finger to his lips.

"Sorry, sir, but I can't find any more places to put people! Your house might be large, but there's not that much bunk space."

"Did you move the dining table like I said?"

"Sir, it seats sixteen people! I can't move it by myself! I told you we needed some more volunteers—"

"And I told you to call the sheriff's department."

"I did! They said they'd send someone over, but—"

The ringing of the doorbell made her jump.

"Impeccable timing," said Pressler.

"What if it's more people seeking shelter?!"

"Build an igloo."

The short walk to the front door was slightly impeded by adults laden with cushions and sleeping bags moving to and fro, children roughhousing, and a growing line for the downstairs bathroom. Brenda attempted to wend her way through the foot traffic and found herself gridlocked halfway across the front hall. Pressler avoided this trap by sidling along the wall. Thus he made it to the entrance first and answered the door. "Deputy James, welcome!"

The deputy glowered at him.

"Or is it Deputy Derrick? I'm sorry, I'm always forgetting."

Never gets old, Pressler thought, finding momentary relief in Derrick's torment.

"Read the badge, sir." Deputy Derrick strode past him irritably.

"And Deputy Benno!" Pressler smiled charmingly at the next deputy who entered.

Benno nodded curtly. "Mr. Mayor."

"You have no idea how good it is to see you both. Thank you very much for—coming." The charm fizzled out as he beheld the third person standing at the door.

"Mr. Mayor," Violet said politely.

Behind him, Pressler caught snatches of gasps and excited whispers: *"It's her!" "The Memory Girl!"* But he kept his eyes on Violet. "How kind of you to volunteer to help," he said, deadpan.

With shoulders squared, Violet looked down at his feet, then back to his face. "May I?"

Pressler then realized that he'd shifted such that his body was blocking the doorway. For a long moment, he didn't move, his eyes locked on Violet's.

Then he pivoted and made a long-armed gesture. "Please."

Violet entered Pressler's house.

* * *

The first thing Cy noticed was the smell. As she entered the community center with her mother and the other volunteers who had come along, they found themselves enveloped in a strong aroma of cooking vegetables. It must have emanated from the back kitchen, as the main room was empty save for a lone figure huddled in the corner under a blanket, surrounded by duffel bags. Whoever it was appeared to be asleep.

A man emerged from the kitchen. Cy recognized Rabbi Metz. "Tables!" he called out as soon as he saw the deputy, before she could say anything. "We need tables along this wall, lined up from there to there. We've got hungry people arriving for lunch any minute." He opened the door of a large closet. "Just use the long ones, not the round ones, or we'll run out of space." With that, he disappeared back into the kitchen.

"Well, you heard him," said Jen. "Let's get to work."

It didn't take them long to set up the tables. Once done, they started putting out the chairs. Rabbi Metz came back out sporadically to have them rearrange things so that the cots—soon to be delivered, in theory—could occupy the bulk of the room.

Shelter seekers began to arrive before the cots did. Like the person sleeping in the corner, they lined up against the walls, laden with hastily collected belongings. Stacks of plates and bowls were set out by the kitchen doorway, and the rabbi directed a buffet line. Those waiting to eat seemed too deep in shock to speak, but once they sat down together, it became clear they had a lot to say. Everyone had sighted some form of destruction by the storm. Some repeated stories of incidents in other towns. Some people had lost power but still had hot water, or, like the Grogans, still had the ability to cook things on a stove. Some of those who had come for the food and not to spend the night at the shelter began to arrange trades, such as cooked meals for an opportunity to shower.

Jen crouched beside the sleeping figure and gently nudged its shoulder. "Excuse me," she said, "I just wanted to let you know, there's food available if you want it."

The form under the blanket stirred. A muffled voice croaked, "Food?"

"That's right."

The figure wriggled, as if swimming. Jen gently pulled back

the blanket to help the person extricate herself. Then she gave a start. "Oh—Myrna!"

Her childhood friend and Veil's resident eccentric, Myrna Redpath looked at her through bleary eyes and tangled hair. "Oh," she grunted in disgust—and tugged the blanket back over her head.

Rabbi Metz asked Cy to bus dishes and then help with dishwashing. As she approached the kitchen she heard his voice again: "You two are amazing helpers, thank you so much. Will you be back to help with supper? Great. See you at four-thirty." She heard footsteps and paused so she wouldn't collide with the people coming out.

When she saw who they were, her face lit up. "Hey, guys!"

Her classmates, Em and Neesha, turned in surprise. "Oh...hey, Cy," said Em.

Rather than responding, Neesha looked away coldly.

Seeing this threw Cy momentarily, resulting in an awkward pause. When Cy finally opened her mouth to speak, Neesha cut her off: "We were just leaving." She hooked her arm through Em's and led them to the exit.

Cy stared after them, at a loss.

* * *

The kitchen staff at Pressler's home was currently much smaller than that of the community center, as it consisted of just Deputy Benno and one other volunteer.

"Hey!" exclaimed thirty-something Chuck Benz as he flipped another pancake on the stove, "I just realized something!"

"What's that?" Benno removed a pan of muffins from the oven and swiftly replaced it with a casserole dish.

Chuck pointed at Benno and then himself with an animated expression. "Benno—and Benz! Alliteration!"

Benno nodded and gave him a tight-lipped smile. "Neat!" He set the oven timer for twenty-five minutes and watched it slowly count down. "Neat," he repeated under his breath, accenting the *t*.

On the floor above, Violet meandered down the hall, looking into each room. The last time she was here, things had been rather frantic, so she hadn't had a chance to explore. Many of the rooms were occupied by those who sought shelter. One family had wedged in a cot next to the bed so their children would be able to sleep in the same room. At the moment, however, those children displayed no interest in sleeping. They darted this way and that, engaged in some kind of tag game. Violet dodged as they careened in her direction, and smiled after them. "No sliding down the banister!" she heard Brenda shout off in the distance.

She came to a wall cupboard, looked inside, and found all manner of towels, washcloths, and bathmats. She tried the next door and found what appeared to be another bedroom. Surprised no one had claimed it, Violet turned on the light—and saw why: it was filthy. Knowing they needed every spare bedroom available, Violet resolved to clean it, herself, when she got the chance.

A dusty chest sat at the foot of the bed. Violet approached and reached out to open it.

"What are you doing?"

Violet yelped and whipped around.

Pressler lurked in the doorway, scowling.

Recovering her breath, Violet replied, "I'm looking for blankets. We're out downstairs, and a lot of people are going to need them tonight." She gestured to the chest. "Are there any in here?"

Pressler said nothing.

"Well, do you mind if I look?" She lifted the latch.

Pressler slammed his hand down on the lid, startling her again. She hadn't even heard him cross the room.

"Listen to me very carefully," Pressler hissed. "You are not welcome here. I will tolerate your presence for the sake of…well, let's say community spirit. But if you go poking your nose around, violating my privacy, I'll give you reason to regret it."

Violet surprised him by laughing. "You've got to be kidding."

"What do you mean by that?"

"It's just kind of funny," she said without humor, "you warning me against snooping in your house, invading your privacy, when that's exactly what you did to me."

"What are you talking about?"

"While we were away on that camping trip, you broke into the Grogans' house and went through my room, my things."

"I thought it was the serial killer who broke in. I understand he left a burner phone on your pillow, to play cat-and-mouse with you."

Violet shook her head and smirked. "It's no good, Pressler. I know you were there. I'm not going to tell you how I know. But I know."

Pressler tilted his head, eyeing her appraisingly. "Or…maybe you don't know, but you suspect. Maybe you're bluffing to see how I'll react."

"I'm not bluffing. I know you were in my room and I know you injured Cy's cat, Roswell."

Pressler narrowed his eyes in suspicion. "I wasn't aware she'd been hurt."

"Now, how would you know the cat's gender?" Violet asked, pointing at him.

Pressler shrugged. "Cyanne must have told me."

"That's interesting, considering Roswell's a boy."

Pressler blinked. "Then I must have mis-remembered."

"That, or you assumed Roswell's a girl 'cause he's a calico. You're right, I was bluffing. I wasn't sure if it was you in my room. Now I am."

Pressler gave her a strange look and a half-hearted laugh. "In case you're unaware, *all* calico cats are female."

"Not if their chromosomes are X-X-Y."

"X-X-Y," Pressler repeated.

Violet shrugged. "I looked it up. All I'm trying to say, Pressler, is that you are in no position to tell me not to go snooping in your home."

They stared at each other, one defiant, the other quietly fuming.

"You'll find some blankets in the cupboard by the laundry room," Pressler finally said in a low voice.

"Thank you, Mr. Mayor."

III

"I'm still mad at you."

"I know," said Jen from the driver seat.

Beside her, Myrna fidgeted impatiently. They were following a plow at five miles per hour. "I can't believe you confiscated all my knives!"

"You shouldn't have had them in the community center to begin with."

"Nobody knew I had them!"

"Myrna, it's you. Everyone knew."

Myrna shrugged, conceding.

They turned onto Mountain Circle. Up ahead they saw Pressler's mansion, one of the only residences with lights on.

"You're sure the food here isn't gonna have any corn?" asked Myrna.

"I told you, Pressler's allergic to corn, just like you are. He's not going to allow it in his house, even under these circumstances."

Myrna grunted. "Never met anyone else who's got the same allergy as me."

"Well, maybe you're related."

Myrna shot her a glare. "If you really want me to forgive you, don't insult me."

III

Jen's jaw tightened as she pulled over in front of the mansion. Once parked, she turned in her seat. "Myrna, I didn't mean to implicate you as the serial killer. It was a misunderstanding. I'm sorry."

Myrna wasn't listening. She was staring at the patrol car already parked in the driveway. "There's another deputy here." She turned to Jen. "Which one is it?"

"There's Deputy Derrick and—"

"Derrick's the one who almost killed me!"

"He didn't try to—"

"When you told him I was the serial killer!"

"Myrna!" Reining herself in, Jen went on more calmly, "I told you, I didn't accuse you. I was speaking to the sheriff on a satellite phone, and the signal cut out. The message he got was incomplete." She sighed. "I know some people saw the scene between you and Derrick. I know they drew the wrong conclusion and they threatened you. That's my fault, and like I said, *I'm sorry.*" She gestured helplessly. "If there's anything I can do to earn back your trust..."

Myrna stared ahead sulkily. "Why do you care?"

"Well, gee, I don't know, Myrna. Maybe because, growing up, you were the only person I could call a friend. Without you..."

"Without me, you would've been the only freak."

"Yeah. Exactly."

Myrna finally looked at her. "Why didn't you tell me you'd moved back to Veil?"

Jen thought back a moment. "Well, you remember what happened right after you found out."

"What?"

"You asked me about my marriage. When I answered you, you knew I was lying."

"Your husband really left you?"

"No, he left Cy. He wanted me to leave with him."

Myrna looked scandalized. "He abandoned his own kid?"

Jen nodded, facial muscles rippling.

"Does she know?"

"She does now." When Myrna didn't respond, Jen went on, "It was hard at first, but her sister and I have been talking with her pretty regularly, and she seems to be doing better. She's applying for an internship with the *Veil Chronicle*. I didn't even know there was such a thing; then I found out Pressler pulled some strings to make it appear. I'm not crazy about him being part of her recovery, but—"

Abruptly and without a word, Myrna got out of the vehicle and shut the door. A moment later, she opened it, said, "I forgive you," and shut it again.

* * *

"Hey, by the way, do you like caramel?"

"Sure." Up to his elbows in soap suds, Benno was growing tired of giving monosyllabic responses to Chuck's non-sequiturs.

"I'm asking 'cause Mom's gonna probably send you a caramel cake. 'Cause I told her you saved my life." He grinned sheepishly. It was the third time he'd brought up Benno's act of heroism.

"Nice."

A few seconds' precious silence, then Chuck went on, "How did you know that door was gonna blow up in my face?"

Benno shrugged with disinterest. "Instinct."

"I still can't believe the serial killer targeted me and I *lived*."

"Yeah."

"I mean, other than Deputy Grogan and that memory girl."

"Yup."

"And that other girl, uh..."

"Trisha."

"And you're the one who caught him!" Chuck nudged him, and Benno dropped a pitcher he'd just rinsed back into the soapy water. "You're, like, the badass of Veil!"

Benno cleared his throat. "Thanks." He threw a glance sideways, hoping to see that the amount of dishes left to wash was miniscule.

"What'd you say?" asked Chuck.

"I said, thanks."

"I thought you said something after that."

"Nope." (Though he had, under his breath.)

Brenda stuck her head in the door. Her hair was gradually working its way free of her ponytail, giving the impression of a gray cloud forming about her head. "Can one of you take a break from kitchen duty and help me?" she breathed.

"Yes." Benno was across the room almost before the dish he'd been holding *plop*ped into the sink full of water.

"Well, before you say yes, I should tell you—"

"No, it's fine, let's go." Benno fairly bulldozed Brenda from the kitchen and shut the door. She led him to the games room, where the pool table dominating the center of the floor made it impractical to place any cots in the room. But at the moment, there was another impracticality.

The room was being destroyed.

Around a dozen children about the age of nine swarmed about the room, wreaking havoc. Two of them were engaged in a sword fight, the swords in this case being pool cue sticks. One child was using a black marker to color in the white squares on a chess board. At least three pairs of legs stuck out from beneath the pool table, and one little girl was on top of it, acting as goalie as her friends tried to roll pool balls into the sockets from the other end.

Benno experienced a brief swell of anxiety, which dissipated once he remembered that the alternative was returning to the kitchen—and Chuck's prattling.

He turned to Brenda. "Is this all of them?"

His bravado made her arch an eyebrow. "We haven't been able to keep track. That's partly why we need a supervisor. Of course their parents are all exhausted."

The eight-ball whizzed through the air dangerously close to Brenda's head, but Benno pivoted and caught the projectile just in time. "They'd probably calm down if we just put a television in front of them."

"Unfortunately Mayor Pressler doesn't have any age-appropriate material."

Benno gave her a quizzical look. "Wait, you're telling me all he has are"—he lowered his voice—"adult films?"

Testily she replied, "Well, I suppose some of them are technically G-rated, but I don't think business economics tutorials are going to do the trick."

"What about the internet?"

"The internet's down. I asked someone who's going to ask somebody else to go and get some form of entertainment, but until then we just need them to *not destroy the house,"* she growled as a cue stick gouged a hole in the wall.

"All right, all right," Benno said soothingly. "Go do what you need to do. I've got this."

Brenda didn't need telling twice.

Alone with the children, Benno felt his anxiety threaten to return. He liked children, but he didn't have all that much experience with them. His former fiancée, Trisha, was the one who had the gift for being able to manage them. If things had gone according to plan, they might have even had their own by now…

BAM. This time the cue stick found a windowpane, in which a hairline crack appeared.

"Oh—kay, everyone!" He had automatically raised his voice, but quickly subverted the sentence into a greeting. Resulting from this, the wielder of the cue stick stopped wielding, Benno had everyone's attention, and none of the kids was scared of him. So far, so good.

"My name's Deputy Benno," he said. A quick scan of the room told him the child who was behaving the least badly was the one building a mile-high stack of checkers. "What's your name?" He asked the child.

"Neil."

"Hi, Neil! How old are you?"

"Nine."

"Is this the first time you've seen an ice storm?" Out of the corner of his eye, Benno noticed the cue-stick fencers still going at it. One of the children playing air hockey with the pool balls abandoned the game and approached Benno, but he pretended not to notice her—yet.

"I remember one when I was five," said Neil, "but we got to stay in our house that time."

"How do you like the mayor's house?" asked Benno.

Neil shrugged.

"I like the mayor's house," said the girl who'd come over.

"Oh, hi," said Benno. "What's your name?"

"Kirsten."

Benno listened to Kirsten's take on the ice storm, then listened to the other children who had approached. In a few minutes, he had learned (or pretended to learn) all their names and had all of them gathered around him, except for the two swinging the cue sticks.

One of the two was clearly starting to lose interest. Pausing the "fight," he said, "I had an uncle who died in an ice storm."

As if he hadn't heard what the boy had said, Benno told him, "If you're done with the sticks, make sure you put them away where you found them." And then he went right back to interacting with the other children.

A minute later, the cue sticks were put away and the last two kids were part of the group.

Great, thought Benno. *Now, all I have to do is find a way to entertain them...*

"Deputy!" All at once Derrick stomped into the room, which instantly quieted. "What do you think you're doing? You're supposed to be in the kitchen."

"I was asked to hang out with these cool kids," Benno explained, avoiding the word "supervise" at the last moment.

Derrick cast his eye over the paused chaos, then looked back at Benno askance. "Exactly who asked you?"

"Brenda, the mayor's secretary."

This brought a change over Derrick's demeanor. "Benno," he said softly, "you do not take instruction from Pressler's lackey. You take your orders from the sheriff."

"Ye-es," Benno replied slowly, "and his orders were for us to help however we can."

"That doesn't mean turning into a yes-man," Derrick hissed.

Benno was growing uncomfortable. He didn't think this was an appropriate conversation to have in front of children.

"Is there really no one else who can babysit?" Derrick demanded.

III

Benno glanced out the door, and luck and inspiration struck at the same time. "Well, the only other choice was..." He gestured.

All eyes turned to the person outside the doorway, just passing by. "Myrna!" Violet caught up to her. "Myrna, I need you to give me back the knife."

"What knife?"

"Come on, Myrna, I saw you take it from the kitchen."

"Well, what am I supposed to use on the kids if they bother me?"

"They're not going to bother you!"

"Try again."

"You could...pretend you have a contagious disease."

Myrna considered this. "Hm. Yeah, I could do that." She handed over the butcher's knife, then noticed the room full of children and two deputies staring at her, and hastened to explain, "When I said, 'use on the kids,' I just meant, scare them."

"Myrna, come on."

"This knife doesn't even really cut through flesh. Here, I'll show you." Before Violet could stop her, she grabbed the knife back and sliced across her palm. "AAAHH!! Aah, I'm bleeding! Oh my god, it hurts! Aaah! Nah, I'm kidding," she laughed, then looked at her hand and did a double take. "Oh, wow, I *am* bleeding." She threw an impressed look at the knife as Violet took it back and herded Myrna away.

Benno gave Derrick a deadpan look.

Derrick harrumphed and exited.

Benno turned to regard the children, several of whom were bug-eyed. Off-handedly he said, "I mean, if you'd rather have her than me..."

* * *

Although he hadn't quite formed a plan of entertainment for the children, Benno decided the first step was to evacuate the games room so that they could inflict no more damage on it. The only other room in the house with enough space that wouldn't be in danger of demolition was the basement—which, being part of a house that belonged to someone wealthy, was not like a basement at all. The kids seemed almost disappointed at the lack of cobwebs, dust, and general creepiness most basements provided.

Benno's first suggestion was that they play a game. However, their antics upstairs seemed to have sapped the kids' interest in competition, leaving them more in the mood for a movie. As this wasn't an option, Benno attempted to use reverse psychology by suggesting he might tell them a story.

This backfired when the children sat down obediently and waited for him to begin.

Masking his panic, Benno tried to stall. "So…what kind of story do you want?"

"Something with lots of violence," said a boy named Chris.

"Violence?" Benno gave him a strange look. "You do realize we all just survived a serial killer who'd been stalking our town for—"

Sparks of mutiny flashed in the eyes of several children.

"Lots of violence, got it." Benno thought frantically to himself, *What kind of story has lots of violence that I can tell to a bunch of kids?* He thought back to his own childhood, and sought for the most violent TV program his parents had let him watch at that age. A memory came to him of a series of black-and-white Charlie Chan movies, shown every Sunday morning on PBS. Many of them involved a series of murders inside a creepy mansion or castle, but the themes were seldom too mature.

III

"Okay," said Benno as ideas began to form in his head. "Okay, um, once upon a time—"

"Also, you should skip descriptions," the girl named Kirsten chimed in. "Like in books, when they describe places and people."

"Skip the descriptions?" Benno repeated doubtfully.

"Yeah, they're boring."

How am I supposed to remember the characters if I don't describe them?

Footsteps thumped on the stairs. Chuck's cheery face appeared. "Hey, you need any help down here?"

"Nope! Thanks, Chuck, I'm good."

"You sure?"

"Yep!"

After Chuck left, Benno started again. "Once upon a time... there was a very rich, very boring man named...Chuck...ton. Chuckton. Benson Chuckton. He owned this huge, really spooky mansion, and one night he—"

A girl named Emma raised her hand. "What's the name of this story?" she asked.

"Uh..." *Lots of violence, lots of violence...* "Uh... 'Kill'... Oh—'Overkill.'"

IV

Benson Chuckton strode briskly into the kitchen. "Mona?" he called.

The cook didn't seem to hear him. She was standing at the far counter, sharpening a carving knife, her back to him.

He approached her. "Mona, the guests will be here shortly. How soon will dinner be—"

All at once, she spun around and leveled the knife at his face, the point nearly shaving off the tip of his mustache. "Very soon," she said in an ominous tone.

"Very good," he stammered and beat a hasty retreat.

As he'd predicted, the guests began to arrive shortly thereafter. Chuckton greeted them at the door one by one. The first to arrive was his next-door neighbor, Doctor Bennodict. Chuckton and Bennodict were not especially close, so when the former invited the latter to a weekend party, Bennodict figured it must be simply out of politeness.

Next to arrive was the famous adventuress, Diane Rogan. Ms. Rogan had had a somewhat close call during her most recent expedition. While camping in the Yukon, she and her two companions had been attacked at night by some large creature—possibly a sasquatch. Ms. Rogan had come away relatively unscathed, but there were perhaps some psychological bruises, which she covered up with bright spirits and cheerfulness.

* * *

One child raised a hand. "What's a sasquatch?"

Benno blinked. "Um, it's another name for Bigfoot."

The kids looked blank. "Like a dinosaur?" asked the boy named Neil.

Benno resisted the urge to comment upon generational gaps. "Ask me later," he said.

* * *

The next two arrivals appeared on the doorstep together, though very much by accident. One was Councilman Elliot Preston, the other was the criminal prosecutor, Sherman DuBois, both of whom were in the running for the upcoming election for governor. Each of them behaved with excessive politeness toward one another in the presence of their host.

These distinguished figures were followed by yet another: Doctor Jennifer Grove, the famous professor of criminology. (In case you're wondering, the reason a boring man like Chuckton had so many rich and famous friends was that he was employed by them all as a financial advisor.)

* * *

From the looks on the kids' faces, they hadn't been wondering.

* * *

Next came a thin, cranky, grumbling man who was disinclined to speak to anyone. His name, apparently, was Dirk, though it wasn't clear whether that was his first name or his last.

Benson Chuckton seemed to be expecting at least one more arrival, but the dinner hour approached and no other guests appeared at the entrance. With a shrug, he turned away from the front door and went to inform his cook of the exact number of places they'd need at dinner.

The doorbell pealed once more.

With a slight smile of satisfaction, Chuckton turned about and answered the door. What he saw wiped the smugness clean from his face. Startled, he took a step back.

Just outside the door stood a woman in shadow. She was not an invited guest, but Chuckton knew who she was.

"Lady Violetta Memory," he breathed.

She stepped into the light and smiled. "Mind if I crash the party?"

* * *

"Why hasn't anybody died yet?"

Many of the kids' eyes were glazed. One was picking at a scab.

Charlie Chan isn't working, thought Benno. *Maybe if I switch to* Murder, She Wrote...

* * *

Suddenly, in the distance, a shot rang out.

It was almost midnight. None of the guests had felt like socializing after dinner, so they'd all gone straight to bed. Each of them had a bedroom of their own.

Doctor Bennodict sat up in his four-poster bed and exclaimed, "Great Scott!" He leaped out of bed, tugged on a dressing gown, and flew out the door.

The wind outside had increased tenfold after sunset, shaking the trees just beyond the ten-foot windows in the corridor. Bennodict could see a crowd gathered around an open door at the far end. "What's happened?" he demanded.

Lady Violetta pivoted toward him and uttered one word in a husky whisper: *"Murder."*

IV

Bennodict gasped. Thunder and lightning crashed. "Quick, let me through," he commanded. "I'm a doctor. I must examine the body."

The crowd parted, allowing him to enter the master bedroom. The bed itself was empty, but a figure sat slumped in an armchair facing the window, its back to the door. Bennodict circled the figure and found himself staring into the lifeless eyes of his host and neighbor, Benson Chuckton.

Wind gusted through the open window. The toupee which had slid down toward Chuckton's eyes was blown across the room, revealing the gunshot wound in the center of his forehead.

* * *

"Bor-ing," said one kid in a singsong voice.

"Hang on," said Benno, "I'm not finished."

* * *

The toupee blew across the room, revealing not only the bullet wound in the center of his forehead, but also a bloody gash on his crown.

* * *

"He was wearing a crown?" asked little Emma.

"No, no, the top of your head is also called the crown," Benno explained.

The children still didn't look satisfied.

* * *

As if the first two mortal wounds weren't enough, Chuckton's throat was also slit from ear to ear.

And his neck was at a strange angle, indicating it was broken.

And to top it all off, someone had driven a fireplace poker straight through his body, skewering him to the chair.

* * *

Benno waited, expecting more complaints.

"Why'd you stop?" asked one child, as wide-eyed as the rest. "Keep going!"

* * *

Elliot Preston wasted no time in casting aspersions on his political opponent. "I have a special gift for reading people," he declared, "and I can tell that you, DuBois, are hiding something!"

Sherman DuBois gave the councilman a mocking glare. "I'll be happy to disclose what I know, now that there's no longer any reason to keep it secret. Chuckton invited me because he wanted to discuss—in private—a legal matter. What that matter was, he didn't tell me, and now he never will."

"Hmm, yes," murmured Jennifer Grove, adjusting her large glasses, "he made a similar overture to me. Said he wanted to consult with me as a criminologist, but wouldn't give any details beyond vague implications. Fascinating."

"Idiots," muttered Dirk.

Mr. Preston turned to him. "You have something to contribute, Mr. Dirk?"

"It's not Mr. Dirk, you moron! Dirk is my first name. Dirk Jordan."

"Very well, Mr. Jordan. What is it you want to say?"

"Instead of hurling petty accusations at each other, you ought to be questioning the one person who wasn't supposed to be here tonight." He pointed a long finger at Lady Violetta.

The mystery woman responded with a cryptic smile. "If you'd like to know why I came here tonight, you need only ask. As it happens, Chuckton invited a friend of mine who couldn't make it, and that friend asked me to attend in her place. I explained this to our host when I arrived, and he deemed it an acceptable arrangement."

IV

"A likely story," Dirk snarled.

"Believe me, if I'd come here to murder Mr. Chuckton, I'd hardly have done it five times."

"Do you chew gum?"

The abrupt, incongruous question came from Diane Rogan, who had just casually picked something up from the floor. Violetta eyed her curiously. "Why do you ask?"

"Because I just found this torn fragment of a label on the floor, and it has the word 'gum.'"

"No, I don't chew gum," replied Violetta. "Perhaps somebody else…?"

None of the others answered in the affirmative.

"Who cares about chewing gum?" grumbled Dirk. "What matters here is why on earth someone decided to attack this man using so many different methods!"

"Not to mention which one actually killed him," remarked the cook. "That's what I'd like to know."

"Well," sighed Dr. Bennodict, rising from where he'd been crouched by the body, "forensics isn't exactly my field, but my guess would be that the first wound to be inflicted was the poker through the abdomen. It certainly wasn't the gunshot that killed him; there's hardly any blood flow from the bullet wound. He could've been dead up to an hour ago."

"You're sure it was the poker that killed him?" asked Violetta.

"Well, no, that just seems to be where the most bleeding occurred." He pointed to the shaft of the poker sticking out just over the belly button. "But it might very well have been one of these other attacks. What's strange is that some of the blood here is wet and some of it is dry. Blood coagulates soon after death, so if the head, throat, and poker wounds all caused bleeding—meaning they were all inflicted within a short period of time—then all of the blood should be wet *or* dry, not some of each. The only explanation is that the window must have been open a long time, and with the increased humidity..."

* * *

One child yawned. Benno had been trying to make the story more interesting, but clearly the forensic details were having the opposite effect. Quickly, he switched it up.

* * *

"Our next order of business," said Mr. DuBois, "is to establish everyone's whereabouts at the time of the gunshot."

"But," protested Dr. Bennodict, "I just explained that the gunshot didn't kill—"

"Please, Dr. Bennodict. Before becoming a criminal prosecutor, I was a police chief. You can trust that in this type of situation, I know the proper procedure."

Bennodict turned to Dr. Grove. "Do you agree with him, ma'am? As a criminologist, I mean."

"Hmm." Dr. Grove adjusted her glasses. "Perhaps I would've recommended a different course of action, but Mr. DuBois certainly has more practical experience than all of the rest of us, so I will defer to his judgment."

"In other words," Violetta whispered to Bennodict, "neither of them has an alibi for the hour before the gunshot."

"As for me," said Mr. DuBois, "when the gun went off, I was running a bath for myself. Immediately after the shot, I turned off the faucet. Mr. Dirk—excuse me, Mr. *Jordan*—since your room is next to mine, may I assume you heard the water in my room stop running?"

Dirk grunted, then said, "That's true."

"How convenient for you," Mr. Preston said to DuBois, his voice dripping with skepticism.

IV

"I was in my room, too," said Dr. Bennodict with realization, "but when I came out to see what the noise was, I didn't see anyone else come out of their rooms."

"Not all of us are able to retire so early," grumbled Mona, the cook. "I was down in the kitchen, still cleaning up."

"I was outside, actually," said Dr. Grove. "I had accidentally left my sleeping pills in my car, and I'd gone out to get them."

"How interesting," said Lady Violetta with a sly smile. "I, myself, was on a second-floor balcony at the time of the gunshot—and I saw no one among the vehicles parked outside."

Dr. Grove promptly replied, "That is hardly surprising, as there is no moonlight to see by with all this cloud cover."

"What were you doing on the balcony?" asked Dirk.

Violetta held up a cell phone. "I was trying to place a call. I thought standing on the balcony might give me better reception."

Mr. DuBois turned to his opponent. "What about you, Preston? Were you in your room, fast asleep, the picture of innocence?"

Mr. Preston heaved a grave sigh. "I heard the gunshot from downstairs, in the billiard room."

"Never took you for an insomniac."

"It wasn't insomnia. I was there avoiding Ms. Rogan. She'd made a pass at me earlier, and she hinted she was going to visit me in my room."

Ms. Rogan's jaw dropped in indignation. "*I* wasn't the one who made a pass at *you!* As if I would flirt with someone so much older than I!"

DuBois smirked as he stifled a laugh.

"I wasn't flirting!" Preston insisted. "I was just giving fatherly advice. Simple benevolence."

"Benevolence can still be creepy. As it happens, when the revolver went off, I was avoiding *him* in the—"

* * *

Benno broke off. What kind of gun had he said it was before? He hadn't! He hadn't specified any kind of gun. Would the kids notice his slip-up? No, but wait, he could use this...

* * *

"Just a minute," Dr. Bennodict cut in. "We don't know what kind of gun fired the shot. You just said, 'revolver.' How do you know what kind of gun it was?"

For a moment, Diane Rogan stood still, wide-eyed. "Well, I—" She stopped, then she started again, "Well, I think I saw a revolver."

"When? Where?" barked DuBois.

"Tonight. One of you had it."

"Who??"

Ms. Rogan frowned. "That's the problem. I can't remember. But it doesn't really matter, does it? If someone were going to shoot a person, he wouldn't use his own weapon. That'd be silly."

"You said, 'he,'" pointed out Violetta. "Was it a man?"

Ms. Rogan thought for a moment, and then she gasped, "Oh! Of course! It was—"

There was a sharp, quick movement, but Mona was quicker. She leapt in front of the exit and brandished a rolling pin, preventing Dirk from making his escape. As Mr. DuBois seized him, Dr. Grove reached into Dirk's jacket and withdrew a revolver. "I'll take this, if you don't mind." She sniffed the barrel. "Used recently." Examining it further, she reported, "One shot fired."

"Something you want to tell us, Dirk?" asked Mr. Preston.

"All right!" Dirk snarled. "I was the one who shot him. You all came running so fast, I didn't have time to ditch the gun. But I didn't kill him! He was dead before I shot him!"

"I already explained that," Dr. Bennodict muttered under his breath.

"When I was younger, I was part of a…an activist group. Some might call it a cult. Today I'm the CEO of a toy-making company. If the press learns about my past, my company's finished. Chuckton knew about it; he was blackmailing me. When I went to bed, I found a note he'd left on my pillow. He was about to double the amount I was paying him. I had to kill him! But he was already dead when I shot him! It was so dark, I just didn't notice till after I'd fired!"

"Nonsense!" rumbled DuBois. "You can't seriously expect us to believe that *more* than one of us contemplated murdering our host tonight."

"Why not?" asked Lady Violetta. "My friend, whom I told you about, was also being blackmailed by Chuckton. I came here on her behalf as a private investigator, to try to find a way to stop him. If two of his invited guests were his blackmail victims, then perhaps the rest…?"

If anyone had spoken immediately following this scandalous supposition, denouncing it as ludicrous, perhaps the idea might have been discarded forthwith. But one and all hesitated, and in doing so, they shared a collective horror.

"I imagine this dinner party was Chuckton's way of telling you all that you couldn't escape the hold he had over you," Violetta mused.

"My god!" exclaimed the cook. "Then any one of you might have killed him! I should never have taken this position! I should've taken that job at the hotel restaurant."

"Well, actually, I'm not being blackmailed," Dr. Bennodict hastened to correct her. "My only relation to Chuckton is that I'm his next-door neighbor. I had no idea—"

"But why would he invite you, then?" asked Ms. Rogan ingenuously.

* * *

"What does 'ingenuous' mean?" asked Emma.

Benno was about to answer when a gruff voice said, "Unsuspecting. Innocent."

Benno looked up and was startled to see Myrna sitting on a crate at the back of the room. She had a plate of food on her lap. Moreover, half a dozen other adults had accumulated in the same area, all listening intently to the story. Benno had been peripherally aware of people coming and going in the background for tools and supplies, but he hadn't thought any of them were paying close attention to him, let alone staying to listen.

His bewilderment must have registered on his face. "Radio's not working," Myrna said with her mouth full, by way of explanation.

"Oh," said Benno.

* * *

"Mr. Chuckton didn't want any of you to realize that the other guests were also being blackmailed," said Lady Violetta. "He wanted each of you to think you were the only one. My guess is that Dr. Bennodict's function was to make this falsehood more plausible—a better sell, so to speak."

"That may be true," said Mr. Preston, "but if that's the case, how do we know *he's* the decoy?"

"Oh, please," drawled Mr. DuBois. "Are you trying to tell us the decoy is you?" He pointed at him. "I heard a rumor that you had an extramarital affair that resulted in a child! Is that what Chuckton blackmailed you over?!"

* * *

To Benno's surprise, none of the kids asked about the meaning of "extramarital affair."

* * *

"How dare you!" roared Preston. "You want to talk about rumors? What about the rumor that you're a bigamist? You can't pretend you have no skeletons in your closet when you accuse others—"

"Gentlemen," broke in Dr. Grove. "I must insist you break off this quarrel—and direct your attention to the blood on Mr. DuBois's sleeve."

DuBois looked at the red spatters on his cuff, and his face went white.

"It was you," breathed Preston.

"No!" DuBois was shaking. "I didn't kill him. Although…like Mr. Jordan, I tried to. I came into this room and I—I snapped his neck. But that's when I noticed the blood, the poker through his chest… He was already dead, I tell you!"

"Wait," said Dr. Bennodict. "You mentioned the poker. What other wounds had been inflicted?"

"I don't know! It was too dark to see!"

"Perhaps we should ask Mr. Preston," Ms. Rogan suggested accusingly.

"What do you mean by that?"

"Ever since we came into this room, you've been glancing at that stone bookend on the mantle with a worried look on your face. What do you want to bet there's blood on it?"

Bennodict went over to the mantle, picked up the bookend, and examined it. "She's right."

"Fine!" Preston exploded. "So I brained him! But I'm in the same boat as these two. He was dead already. I'm no more a murderer than they are."

"That leaves the poker and the throat-slitting," murmured Bennodict. "I wonder what weapon was used for that."

"I think Dr. Grove can tell us that," said Dirk.

Dr. Grove gave him a look over the rim of her glasses. "Oh?"

"Like Mr. Preston here, you've been throwing guilty glances over at that vase on the windowsill."

"I'm sure I've done no such thing."

Bennodict removed the flowers from the vase and, using a handkerchief, extracted a sharp kitchen knife.

"That's one of my knives!" Mona cried out indignantly.

Dr. Grove sighed. "Very well. Like the others, I came into this room to murder our host, and acted on my intention only to discover that he'd been killed some time before."

"Why?" asked Ms. Rogan.

"As an eminent criminologist, I must preserve my reputation. That reputation would be utterly destroyed should it get out that my former husband was a criminal, and that I was aware of it—or, even worse, that I was *not* aware of it."

"When you, uh—attacked him," said Dr. Bennodict, "what wounds had he sustained?"

"His head had not yet been damaged, but the poker was sticking through his chest. I don't know if his neck had been broken."

"Then if everyone's been telling the truth, the poker must have been the first attack and the actual cause of death."

"That makes sense," agreed Ms. Rogan. Then she noticed everyone staring at her. "What?"

"What were *you* blackmailed for?" inquired Mr. Preston.

IV

"Oh. Do I have to say?"

No one answered.

"Well, the truth is, I'm not really Diane Rogan. I mean, I *am*. I'm just not *that* Diane Rogan. She and I met in a bar in Hong Kong, and we discovered we had the same name. Then she was killed in a bar fight, and I didn't have any money, so I just assumed her identity. She'd told me all about her adventures, so I wrote a book and made a lot of money."

"Maybe you were running *out* of money, and Chuckton put pressure on you to pay him more," accused Mr. DuBois.

Ms. Rogan frowned. "Well, that's the strange thing. He'd never put pressure on me before. But tonight, out of the blue, he told me he was doubling his 'fees.'"

"When did he say this to you?" asked Dr. Bennodict.

"He didn't tell me in person. He left me a note, just like he did for Mr. Dirk."

"Jordan!"

"Whatever."

Lady Violetta stepped forward, her eyes agleam with curiosity. "What exactly did your note say?"

"Just that I'd have to pay double from now on, or he'd expose me as a fraud."

Violetta looked at Dr. Grove, Mr. Preston, and Mr. DuBois. "Did you all receive notes as well?"

They all said they had.

"And did they all specifically reference the secret for which he was blackmailing you?"

"What has that got to do with it?" asked Preston. "Chuckton obviously wanted to squeeze us all for more money, so who can blame us for what we tried to do? Whoever really did kill him did the rest of us a favor!"

"But what if Chuckton *wasn't* doubling his fees?" Lady Violetta persisted.

"But, the notes—"

"I don't think he wrote them."

"What?!" exclaimed Dr. Bennodict. "Why not?"

"Because I received one, myself."

Everyone stared her with renewed suspicion. In a mild voice Dr. Grove said, "I thought you told us you were *not* one of Chuckton's blackmail victims."

"Exactly," said Violetta. "Which is why it puzzled me. But my note was different from all of yours. It said, 'Double fees from now on or I expose your secret.' Don't you see? Unlike the notes you received, mine was generic, not specifying my dark secret. Almost as if..." She turned to regard the dead man. "As if the writer of the note *believed* I was a blackmail victim, though they didn't know what for."

"But why?" asked Dr. Bennodict. "Why write fake, threatening notes? What was their purpose?"

"To provide the victims with an impetus to eliminate their blackmailer. Or at least to induce one of them to attempt murder. She probably didn't intend for *four* of them to comply."

"'She?' You mean—?" Mr. Preston pointed at Ms. Rogan.

"I mean..." Violetta pivoted. "Mona Redding, earlier you lamented not taking another job. Exactly how long have you had this one?"

The cook stuttered, "Well, not very long, I suppose. What does it matter?"

"It matters because if you knew about Mr. Chuckton's blackmail scheme, then you were in an ideal position to plan his murder and throw suspicion onto others. You planted the notes, stabbed Chuckton with the poker, and then all you had to do was wait for at least one blackmail victim to come along and attempt murder, thus incriminating all of the victims."

"But why kill him, herself, if she expected others to?" asked Dr. Grove.

"In case her plan failed, and no one succumbed to the temptation of murder."

"But why would she do it?" demanded Dr. Bennodict. "Chuckton wouldn't have hired her if he were blackmailing her, would he?"

"No, I don't think he was blackmailing her." Violetta stepped closer to Mona. "But perhaps he targeted someone close to her. Someone who couldn't endure the torment. Someone she promised to avenge. Am I right?"

Mona had closed her eyes. When she opened them, they were filled with tears. Letting out a scream of rage, she charged at the others, trying to get to the door. After a brief struggle, they subdued her, locked her in a storage closet, and waited for the police to arrive.

* * *

Benno drew a deep breath, relieved he'd finally reached the end, and quite impressed with himself for making up such a long story as he'd told it. He hoped his audience was satisfied with his conclusion.

The children were frowning. One of them said, "How come only one person's died so far?"

V

Cy had no idea how she would've managed all these children at the community center if someone hadn't brought out a DVD player and hooked it up to a TV. Without entertainment, she couldn't imagine keeping the kids in line. They were almost to the end of the first season of *Avatar: The Last Airbender,* but they'd be breaking for dinner soon.

The adults were spread out among the cots. A few were sleeping, some had set up makeshift work stations with laptops and papers spread around them, and one man had his arm around his partner, who was quietly weeping.

It was still the afternoon, though it had grown dark outside. The precipitation was supposedly over; all that remained was a billowing wind. Cy felt it as the door opened and shut again.

She jumped up when she saw who'd just entered. She glanced at the children; they all seemed too mesmerized to get into any trouble if she left them unsupervised for a moment.

Em and Neesha stopped in their tracks when they saw Cy approaching.

Cy slowed to a halt and gave an awkward wave. "Hey, guys," she said uncertainly.

As before, Em's eyes betrayed discomfort while Neesha's were cold, resentful. "What do you want?" she said.

V

Cy shook her head helplessly. "What's going on with you two? Why are you...?"

Neesha continued to stare at her icily. Em said, "We're just—confused."

"About?"

"About why you're getting help from Pressler. With the internship at the newspaper office. Why would you let him help you after...after he—"

"After he hired those men to rob his own house," snapped Neesha, "and they kidnapped us because we happened to be in the way."

Cy gasped in realization. "Oh my god..." She covered her mouth. "I am so sorry, guys, I didn't even think about how it would make you feel. I—"

"How *we* feel?!" Neesha exclaimed, remembering at the last moment to keep her voice down. The man comforting his partner turned his head and frowned at them. Neesha stepped forward and whispered, "Cy, the question is, how can *you* feel okay about it? How can you even be okay just being *around* him? You were the one who told us the truth about what he did. You told us about him probably being a criminal in the past—maybe even a criminal *now*."

"Look," said Cy, "there's stuff going on with my family that I haven't told you guys. I haven't really told anybody; I'm still dealing with it. When I first found out, I went to Pressler for help—"

"You what?!" Em went bug-eyed.

"No—no, I—I went to him because I thought he'd have the resources to—to... I told him he owed me—owed *us* for—"

"Cy, Cy, stop." Neesha took a deep breath. "We don't care why you went to him in the first place. What we want to know is why you're still going to him, acting like he's a normal guy—and not a criminal."

In a softer voice, Em said, "It's like…you're acting as if what happened…never happened."

Cy opened her mouth to protest. Then she thought to herself, *Why am I still letting him help me?* Was it because he'd become a replacement father figure? No, it wasn't that. Finally, an answer came to her: *Because he won't ever leave. He won't abandon me. Or if he did, it wouldn't hurt as much.* And she realized she believed it to be true. As shady as Pressler was, he'd instilled a sense of trust in her. She knew, in her heart, that whatever else he might do, he would always do what he thought was right by her. No matter what anyone else in her life might do to hurt her, he was the one person who could be relied upon.

How could she explain that? She knew at once that she couldn't. Was losing two of her best friends worth a feeling of safety? Of course it wasn't. She could learn to put her trust in people who were more deserving of it.

"You know what?" she said. "You don't have to worry about it anymore. I won't apply for the internship. I'll call him and tell him thanks, but no thanks." She smiled.

Neesha huffed. "So if you didn't have to kiss up to us, you'd stay with him."

"What?" Cy stammered, but Em and Neesha had already shouldered past her and disappeared into the kitchen. They didn't even look back.

A disturbance broke out among the children. The episode they'd been watching had ended, and the remote control that could start the next episode was being fought over.

Cy, having sunk onto the nearest cot, took no notice.

* * *

V

"What do you mean, we haven't found the real killer?!" cried Dr. Bennodict. "You and I were both there when she confessed!"

"She confessed to stabbing Mr. Chuckton, yes," Lady Violetta patiently explained, "but like the other attempted killers, she claims he was already dead."

"Preposterous!"

"She also denies writing and leaving the fake blackmail notes. Remember, Mona was the one who asked you to determine which murder method was the actual cause of death. Why would she do such a thing if *she* had inflicted that wound?"

"But the poker *was* the cause of death!"

"Are you sure? Could he not have been dispatched by some other means, which we have not detected?"

"Like what?"

"Was he, perhaps, smothered?"

"Smothered?!" exclaimed Dr. Bennodict. "What ever gave you that idea?"

"I noticed that the aesthetic in Mr. Chuckton's room is symmetry, marred only by the absence of one of two cushions on the window seat."

"You're suggesting somebody murdered him by placing a *cushion* over his face? My dear lady, the idea is laughable. For one thing, our host was a *large* man. I find it highly unlikely that one of us would be able to overpower him in such a manner. Furthermore, I found no traces of skin discoloration, fabric in his mustache, or any other evidence that the cause of death was not the poker through his abdomen. And despite what you've told me, I see no reason not to believe that the person who has confessed to wielding said poker is guilty of the crime. The only thing that could possibly persuade me otherwise is if there were a second—"

A shrill scream echoed in the distance.

"Victim," breathed Dr. Bennodict.

The two of them ran headlong toward the sound, which seemed to have come from the kitchen. Others joined them along the way.

When they reached the kitchen, one and all gasped in horror, for there they found...Ms. Rogan.

* * *

"Nooo!" Emma wailed. "Not Ms. Rogan! I like her!"

"You didn't let me finish," Benno quickly lied.

* * *

They found Ms. Rogan...standing over the dead body of...

"Dirk Jordan!" Dr. Bennodict exclaimed.

All six occupants of the room were shocked, but not just at the discovery of a second victim.

"Is that—" began Dr. Grove.

"Are those—" gasped Mr. Preston.

"Does he have—" stuttered Mr. DuBois.

"Yes," confirmed Dr. Bennodict after a cursory examination, lifting the body's stubby fingers to inspect the corpse more closely. "He has the exact same wounds as Mr. Chuckton."

It was true. The dead man's head was smashed, his neck broken, his throat slit, and there was a hole in his chest, made by a fireplace poker. The only difference was that this man had not been shot.

Even Lady Violetta was at a loss for words.

"I came down for a midnight snack," Ms. Rogan said faintly. "I heard a noise in here before I came in, but I didn't see anyone."

Violetta glanced at the door leading to the dining room.

"The freezer door was ajar. I opened it, and..." She gestured to the dead man sprawled before the large freezer.

V

"It was the cook!" proclaimed Mr. Preston as Mr. DuBois ran off to check on the makeshift holding cell. "She's escaped, and she's trying to bump off the rest of us!"

"Not unless she managed to poison Mr. Jordan before we imprisoned her," Dr. Bennodict refuted as he further inspected the body.

"Poison?!" Dr. Grove knelt next to him interestedly.

"Yes, see the cyanotic discoloration here around the lips? The mark of a syringe here on the neck? I suspect that if the rest of the face were visible, there would be further telltale signs."

"How extraordinary," murmured Lady Violetta.

Mr. DuBois returned, out of breath. "Ms. Redding is still secure," he reported.

"Why would the murderer have hidden the body in the freezer?" asked Mr. Preston.

"Undoubtedly to obscure the time of death," answered Dr. Grove, touching the back of the victim's neck and quickly drawing her hand away.

"I think the more obvious question," said Dr. Bennodict, "is why the second victim was attacked with the same implements as Mr. Chuckton."

"And why didn't the murderer leave the weapons at the scene?" said Lady Violetta, peering at the hole in the victim's chest.

The suspects looked at each other.

In a group, they returned to the first crime scene. The knife and bookend lay on the coffee table in the exact same spots they'd been left earlier, and the poker once again skewered their host to his chair.

"That's grotesque!" burst out Ms. Rogan, shuddering.

"Our murderer has a sick sense of humor," observed Mr. DuBois.

"I disagree," said Lady Violetta.

"You find this humorous?" asked Dr. Bennodict, appalled.

"Not at all. I don't think humor was the intended purpose."

"Then what?" asked Mr. Preston.

Violetta shrugged. "Why does anyone ever do anything outrageous?" When no one spoke, she, herself, responded, "Because they have to. Because they have no other choice."

Dr. Grove stared at her. "You sound as if you know who the killer is."

Violetta smiled her sly smile. "I believe I do."

Ms. Rogan gasped. "Who??"

"The one who planned this crime down to the last detail."

"Who?" asked the rest of them.

"The one who was willing to kill to protect their secret."

"Who??!"

"The one we'd never suspect."

"Who?!!!"

"The one who—"

* * *

"Excuse me, everyone!"

Necks craned as the audience turned to see Violet waving from the doorway at the back of the room. "Hi. Sorry to interrupt the story, but dinner is just about ready, and Brenda asked me to make sure everyone comes to eat right away so she can be certain everyone gets fed."

A chorus of "Aww"s came from the children. Turning to Benno, one asked, "Can't you just tell us who did it?"

"Well, that's gonna take some time to explain," said Benno, "but don't worry. We can finish the story after you guys eat. Besides, this way, you have a chance to try and figure out the mystery for yourselves."

V

"You promise you'll finish?" asked Emma.

Benno gave her a beaming smile. "Promise."

The kids shot through the gaps in the crowd and up the stairs, followed by the adults, leaving Benno by himself in the basement. Benno rose from his chair, but instead of following the others, he took a few steps forward, sat on the floor, and then lay on his back, arms outstretched.

His voice was hoarse from talking so much, so when he spoke, he whispered:

"I'm doomed."

* * *

"Mr. Mayor?"

Elijah Pressler had heard those two words so many times today—invariably followed by grim tidings—that, despite how long and how hard he'd worked to acquire the title, he'd come to despise the sound of it. "What?" he growled.

Brenda hesitated. "Um...I was just wondering if you wanted to say a few words before everyone digs in."

From his desk chair in his study, Pressler leveled a dead-eyed stare in her direction. "Brenda, I know you're tired, but that is an incredibly stupid idea. These people are stressed and hungry, and you're suggesting we force them to *wait* while I make some platitude-filled speech before they're allowed to eat. Are you trying to make them hate me?"

"No—I'm sorry, sir, I just thought—"

"Is there anything that *needs* my attention?" Pressler cut her off, uninterested in her apology.

"No, no, there's nothing. I mean, well..."

"What?"

"Th-the fireplace in the east lounge is out of firewood, and there's still a problem with the radiators, so the room's getting cold. There's one man who says he has experience chopping wood, but he's starving, so he won't do it till after dinner. Myrna Redpath also has experience, but I don't feel comfortable giving her access to more cutting implements. She's already tried to steal three kitchen knives—"

Pressler stood up. "I'll do it."

"Oh, sir, are you sure? It could be dangerous out—"

Pressler marched right by her, not even bothering to respond.

After donning his winter attire, he took a circuitous route to the back door, thereby avoiding the dining room. Once outside, he glimpsed his guests through the window. He paused for a moment, observing the community that was forming inside his house. For community it was, not like the parties he'd thrown in the past, where guests separated themselves into groups and cliques. Despite their circumstances, the guests staying in his home tonight seemed happier than any he'd had before.

He hurried on to the shed where he kept his axes, stumbling on the way and nearly falling into the pond behind his house, which was frozen over with ice.

One after another, he laid logs of firewood on the chopping block, raised the axe and swung it down, cleaving the wood in two. He took satisfaction in the uncomplicated physical work. At the end of a day like today, it brought him comfort like nothing else could. Not even the cold bothered him. In fact, he barely felt it.

"Who is she then?"

The axe froze in mid-swing.

"The girl with no memory of her past possesses a secret that will shake the town of Veil to its core. It's her destiny to bring down a great evil that's festered here for years."

Pressler turned in place, knowing what he would see.

V

Violet stood behind him, holding a certain laptop, the source of the recorded voices. *"Someone's here! Someone followed us! Followed you!"*

"No one followed me!"

They were the voices Rob Mulroy and Tuck Fleagle, the reporter and his informant. Keeping her accusing eyes on Pressler, Violet let the recording play out until they heard the gunshot that killed Mulroy, heard his body slump to the ground, heard Fleagle run off in terror, never to be seen or heard from again. Then she stopped the playback. "I found what you were hiding," she said. She set the laptop on a nearby stump. "It was you. *You* leaked this recording to the public. Why? What did you get out of it?"

Pressler stared at her coldly and said nothing.

"How did you even get hold of it? The sheriff had the only copy."

Pressler's voice was icily quiet. "You'd better join the others for dinner before it gets cold."

Violet ignored him. She seemed to be thinking out loud. "You leaked the recording the same night we discovered the bodies of Rob Mulroy and Matt Foley. I thought it was the serial killer who leaked it—to start a panic in the town. Is *that* why you did it? To cause a panic? To turn everyone against the sheriff for keeping the murders a secret? To win more voters in the election for mayor?"

"You don't want to go down this road." From his tone, it sounded as if Pressler expected his words to fall on deaf ears.

"Wait a minute," said Violet, "I've been assuming you knew about the bodies found in the car before you released the recording. What if you didn't? What if that was just a coincidence?"

"Violet..."

"On the recording, Mulroy and Fleagle don't say anything about the murders. They only talk about me. The fact that Mulroy was killed made it seem like *I* was connected to the murders."

"Well, maybe you are. We still don't know why these killings happened. The murderer hasn't told us. Maybe I was trying to warn Veil that you're a danger to us all."

Violet shook her head in disgust. "You are so full of it. At that time, you didn't consider me a hindrance to your business. This wasn't about me." She ticked off her fingers one at a time. "So if we take away me, the serial killer, and the bodies found that night, all that's left...is Rob Mulroy's murder."

Pressler's breath was visible in the frosty air, so he kept it under control as best he could.

"I'm getting close, aren't I," said Violet with a smirk. "There's something else you're hiding. Wait—that's it! You leaked the recording as a *distraction* from something else! Because the recording isn't as important as it seems! No, that's not it... Or—it's misleading! Rob's death had nothing to do with me *or* the serial killer! Except he was one of the victims...unless he—wasn't..."

Pressler closed his eyes.

All the color drained from Violet's face. "Oh my god..." She took a step back, then seemed to freeze in place. "You—*you*... had him killed."

Pressler opened his eyes and regarded her unblinkingly.

Violet seemed to become aware of the axe he held at his side, yet she remained still. "You leaked the recording just to draw suspicion away from yourself."

Pressler's nostrils flared in anger. "From *myself?* Jen Grogan was never supposed to go looking for Rob Mulroy. She and that rookie deputy were drawing too much attention to his disappearance. I didn't know his *body* was going to turn up, but I did know that sooner or later, suspicion would fall on Cyanne and her mother. Do you think it never occurred to me that if Mulroy died, they'd become the prime suspects?!"

He'd taken a step toward her. Reflexively she took one step back. "Is that why you did it?" she asked. "Because of what Rob did to Cy?"

Pressler took another step. Violet compliantly did likewise. "There were other reasons," he said. "Before attacking me in public, Rob wanted me to hire him, put him on my publicity team. When I turned him down, he dug into my affairs and threatened me with an exposé."

Another step forward. Another step back.

"You could've dealt with him in other ways," said Violet.

Pressler drew in a deep breath through his nose and let it out slowly. "You're right. I could have. I suppose there really was only one reason after all." His eyes bore into hers, hypnotizing her.

She blinked, attempting to resist. "I—I care for her, too, you know."

"Then don't pretend you're sorry he's dead."

Step. And step.

"I won't. You're the one who's pretending. You want to believe you're a protector. But you're a murderer."

Pressler scoffed. "It must be so convenient for you, having amnesia."

"Convenient!?"

"It's easy to stand there being vindictive when your moral ledger's been wiped clean."

This time she didn't step back. Her lower jaw jutted forth. "If I ever find out I'm guilty of a crime, I'll hold myself accountable."

"Hah!" barked Pressler. "Of course you will. Until then, forgive me if I consider you a hypocrite."

Violet turned on her heel. "Why am I even talking to *yaaaahhhh!!!"* She'd backed up so far that her steps had taken her to the middle of the icy surface of the pond. One step more and she'd broken straight through, submerging instantly.

With a sigh, Pressler strolled back to the chopping block and carefully set the axe beside it, leaning the handle against the edge. He paid no attention to the splashing and sputtering behind him.

"Pressler! Help! Please! H-help me!"

He started to gather the chopped firewood in a wheelbarrow.

"HELP!" Her voice was too choked by freezing cold to reach any ears but his.

Pressler shivered. The cold had permeated his layers and he was starting to feel it.

"Pres..." Violet's voice had dwindled to nothing more than an agonized squeak. "Please..."

Pressler hesitated, then he turned his head toward her with a look of detachment.

Flakes of ice had already formed on Violet's eyelids. Her hand shook as she extended it toward him.

Pressler might as well have been frozen, himself.

"You...bast..." Violet's lips froze mid-word. With one last gurgle she slipped through the hole she'd made in the ice, first face, then arm, and last of all her fingers, still clawing for purchase. Then she was gone.

With the air of having been relieved of a long-suffered burden, Pressler gave a slow exhalation, watching his breath turn into a puff of moisture. He finished loading the firewood into the wheelbarrow, collected the laptop Violet had brought along, and began wheeling it all toward the house.

Knock. Knock. Knock.

The wheelbarrow halted. Pressler turned his head in increments. Part of him felt shame at his hesitation; the other part rebelled against what he'd just heard.

The icy surface of the pond looked just as it had a moment ago. Within an hour the hole would likely be frozen over.

Giving his head a little shake, Pressler continued pushing the load along the path.

KNOCK.

The wheelbarrow slipped from his hand.

KNOCK.

He whipped around.

KNOCK.

He stood still a few more seconds, then marched back over to the pond.

The ice sheet was opaque. The water beneath the hole was dark. There was nothing to see.

No, wait—the ice was changing, its surface turning from white to glassy, like mist fading in the early morning. He could see beneath the ice.

He could see Violet.

Her dark hair fanned about her head as she slowly sank, the purple streak shimmering. Her lovely face was unnaturally pale, almost peaceful in death. One would never guess her demise had been brought about intentionally.

Her eyes opened.

Before Pressler could draw back, her arm shot upward, her fist drove through the ice, and Pressler felt her stinging, icy fingers close around his throat, crushing his windpipe. Then she sank like a stone, the chilly water engulfing the man as she dragged him under.

Her eyes were still locked with his, and they were the last things he saw as light and feeling dimmed around him, then darkened.

VI

"Violet, are you okay?"

Violet gave a start. She'd brought her dinner into the game room to eat in solitude, but she'd become lost in thought. Her food sat untouched on the pool table.

"Yeah," she said to Deputy Benno. "I'm fine, just a little shaken up. How's Chuck?"

Benno shook his head in amazement. "Chuck is…a champ. He's sitting by the fire under about twelve blankets, and he's drunk six cups of hot cocoa, but still… I'll be honest, I don't know if I could've done what he did."

"I know *I* couldn't have. Diving under the ice like that…to save Pressler…"

"Well, it's lucky you were looking out the window and saw Pressler when he fell into the pond," Benno remarked. "You deserve credit for saving him just as much as Chuck."

Violet shivered. "If I hadn't looked at just the right moment…" She felt Benno lay a comforting hand on her shoulder. She turned to him. "Is he gonna be all right?"

"I'm sure he'll be fine. His lungs definitely weren't damaged too badly. When the paramedics loaded him into the ambulance, he was delirious. I could hear him shouting about a dead girl pulling him under the ice."

Violet trembled, then shook herself. "I can't eat right now." She pushed the plate away. "I wish there were something else for me to do, something I could help with."

Benno bit his lip. "We-ell…"

She looked at him expectantly. "Yes, Benno?"

He sucked in air through his teeth and said in a low voice, "I'm in desperate need of help."

"With?"

"My story."

"Your st—" Violet did a double take. "You mean that mystery story you've been telling?"

"I—don't know how to end it! Or who the murderer is!"

Violet covered her mouth to stifle her laughter.

"Look, I've been making it up as I go. I *had* an ending that made sense, but the kids made me keep going! I just kept inventing details to keep it interesting, and now I can't remember it all!"

The dam broke. Violet snorted and rocked with mirth. Then, to Benno's great surprise, she spread her arms and hugged him, still laughing. Forgetting his troubles for a moment, Benno hugged her back. When they pulled apart, both were laughing.

"Seriously, though," said Benno, "if I don't give these people a satisfying ending, they're gonna eat me alive."

Violet gave him a smile that was half exasperation, half amusement. "Benno, you took down Veil's serial killer—after sustaining, like, ten severe injuries."

"Five," Benno corrected automatically.

"And you're worried about audience approval ratings? They're not listening to be entertained. They're listening because it's *you*. You're a hero. They're probably just too shy to introduce themselves. I know I would be."

Benno was genuinely touched. "Thank you."

"Hmm." Violet stroked her chin pensively. "I didn't really get to hear much of your story, but a lot of people were talking about it at dinner, discussing theories and solutions. I think I've heard enough to be familiar with the plot and characters."

"Really?" said Benno, impressed.

"Yeah." She gave him a wry look. "'Lady Violetta Memory?' Seriously?"

Benno gave a nervous laugh.

"You sure you didn't have a specific ending in mind?"

"Nnnope."

"Because, thinking it over, I can only see one possible answer."

* * *

Cy had thought that sitting on the bench by the community center's side exit would give her a bit of privacy. Unfortunately, she hadn't accounted for multiple people stepping outside for a smoke. Cy could not understand how smoking was still a thing, it was so repulsive. But what truly vexed her was the fact that every time someone passed through the door, it swung closed with a long, annoying *creak*. She considered finding a different place to think, but perhaps the stream of comers and goers had finally run out—

Creak.

Cy winced and put her hands over her ears. Although she knew someone had just come outside, she couldn't help but let a sob escape her throat.

"Cy?" It was her mother. Jen sat by her side and put her arm around her. "Hey. We're going home in just a minute. It's been a long day. I'm really proud of you."

Cy nodded, sniffling, not looking directly at her. "I'm okay," she said in a shaky voice.

"What's wrong, honey?"

Cy blew out an unsteady breath. "Have you ever made a mistake and hurt someone, and you wanted a second chance, but they wouldn't give it to you?"

Jen's eyebrows went up. "Mmm, once or twice," she said. After a moment, she went on, "It sucks, but you just have to wait until that person is ready to forgive you. It'll probably take you by surprise when they do."

They sat in silence for a minute.

"I'm not going to apply for Pressler's internship," Cy finally said. "I mean—the newspaper internship."

Jen's eyebrows went up briefly. "Oh. Okay."

"Yeah, I'm sure you're crushed."

Jen chuckled and kissed the top of her daughter's head. "I support you," she whispered. Then she stood. "See you at the car."

She went back inside, and the door began its irritating whine. Cy glared at it, and the door seemed to slow, prolonging the torment. Cy sprang up from the bench, marched to the door and shoved it.

Thud. "Augh!"

"Oh my god!" Cy fumbled for the handle and pulled the door open. "I'm so sorry!"

A teenage boy stood inside, half-doubled over, his hand over his eye.

"Oh God, are you bleeding?"

"No," he gasped, lowering his hand. "I'm fine, it just—" He caught sight of her and blinked. He was an inch or two taller than she, with dark brown hair in a bowl cut. His eyes were strikingly blue. His shoulders were broad, the rest of him lean.

Cy took his abrupt silence as a sign of pain. "Jeez, I'm sorry, where did it hit you? Where's it hurting?" She took his head in her hands and examined him closely.

Apparently realizing he'd stopped speaking, the boy murmured, "It—it's not that bad."

Cy noticed he was blushing. Then she realized how close their faces were and she blushed, too. "Oh, good," she said, releasing him. When he continued to stare at her, unspeaking, she stuck her hand out awkwardly. "I'm Cyanne Grogan."

He shook her hand as if starstruck. "Yeah. I know." He shook himself. "I mean, nice to meet you."

Cy restrained a grin. "I'm hoping you have a name, too."

The boy closed his eyes in apparent self-cursing. "Luther," he said. "I'm Luther. Hennessey."

"Nice to meet you, Luther."

If either of them noticed they were still holding hands, they didn't seem to mind.

* * *

Thunder crashed.

Lightning boomed.

"The murderer," said the intrepid Lady Violetta, "planned this crime very carefully, to make certain of an airtight alibi."

"But none of us *has* an alibi!" protested Mr. DuBois.

"Obviously they didn't plan well enough," remarked Dr. Grove.

"Let her speak," said Mr. Preston.

Violetta went on, "The murderer left notes for all of us in order to induce us to commit murder. Each one of us would find the victim dead but still warm. We'd know that someone else beat us to the kill by just a little bit of time. With each successive attack, the true murder method got harder and harder to discern from the others."

"So…he *was* dead when the cook stabbed him in the chest?" asked Ms. Rogan, looking confused.

Violetta turned her head slowly to stare at a particular person. "I'm surprised you don't object to this…Dr. Bennodict."

"Me? Why would I object?"

"You examined the body. You reported that the poker was sticking through Mr. Chuckton's *abdomen,* not his chest. If I remember correctly, the wound was an inch or two above the belly button, wasn't it?"

"Oh, well, the layman's terms are not typically accurate, so one must allow for—"

"But it *was* in his chest! I remember!" exclaimed Mr. Preston. Dr. Grove and Mr. DuBois concurred.

"How curious," said Violetta. "How can this be? Doctor, you also said that the blood in the vicinity of the body was wet in some places, and in other places dry. You said this could be accounted for by the window being open. But if the window had been open for that long, the wind would've blown the toupee off the dead man's head long before we discovered him! The only possible explanation is that when we heard the gunshot, *the body had only been in that chair a few minutes!"*

The others stared at her in shock.

"But we saw him!"

"We—attacked him."

"No." Violetta shook her head. "All of you said that the room was dark, too dark to see that he was dead. And too dark to see—*that it wasn't Mr. Chuckton at all!!"*

Lightning flooded the room with stark illumination, followed by a thunderclap.

"The people in this room are not the only ones Benson Chuckton blackmailed. One of them found out about the others, and he used what he'd discovered to come up with a plot to kill Chuckton and frame the party guests, so that no one would ever even know he'd been here tonight."

"Wait," said Dr. Grove, "you're saying the killer is someone we haven't even met?"

"Oh, you've met him all right," said Violetta. "Mr. Chuckton introduced him to us all—as Mr. Dirk."

"Dirk Jordan?!" gasped Ms. Rogan. "But he's—"

"No!" shouted Violetta. "*Not* Dirk Jordan. That is the point. Chuckton called him Mr. Dirk because *Dirk really is his surname.* Dirk only told us he was Dirk *Jordan* after Chuckton was dead—*and he was lying.*"

"Why?"

"Because earlier in the day, he'd kidnapped the real Dirk Jordan—who was another one of Chuckton's blackmail victims—and brought him here under sedation. After we all went to bed, he drugged Chuckton, hid him away, and put Dirk Jordan in his place. He killed Jordan by lethal injection, then disguised him as our overweight, mustached host, which explains the missing cushion and the torn fragment of the *spirit* gum label. Then he waited and watched from the shadows as four other people came into the room one at a time and attacked the already-dead man. When it was over, Dirk removed the disguise, put Jordan in the freezer, and replaced Chuckton in the chair. Mr. Dirk killed him using the same methods chosen by you, his decoys—but there was a problem! Even in death, Chuckton was *tall.* Jordan was stabbed in the chest, and the poker had made a hole in the back of the chair. If Dirk stabbed Jordan in the chest, it wouldn't align with the hole. A second hole would be suspicious. So he had to stab him lower—through the *abdomen.*

"He waited a few minutes, then shot Chuckton through the head. When he admitted to doing so later, he gave himself the perfect alibi. As the only person who used the method of attack that was proven ineffective, he was the only one of us whom no one suspected. However, *I* suspected him when I saw that the body hidden in the freezer had short, stubby fingers, whereas Dirk's were long and thin. He intended for Jordan's body to be found in a certain place, but Ms. Rogan interrupted him as he was trying to move it. Still, the result would've been the same. As far as we knew, Dirk Jordan was in this house tonight, and then was found dead. There would never have been any question of a second Dirk. That was the beauty of discovering another blackmail victim whose first name happened to be the same as his last."

* * *

Benno paused for breath.

In the back of the room, over the heads of his audience, Violet gave him two thumbs up.

The adult portion of his audience evidently agreed with her, as, assuming the story was over, they gave Benno a polite round of applause and began to disperse.

The children remained where they were, wearing frowns of puzzlement.

"So...did they catch the killer?" asked Chris.

"Yup," said Benno. "They searched the house and found him, uhm, in the attic."

"What was the killer being blackmailed for?" asked Kirsten.

Benno's brain was tired. "Counterfeiting."

"But then why didn't he just use the counterfeit money to pay the blackmail?"

"Um—"

VI

"How come they thought the body in the freezer was Dirk's?" asked nine-year-old Neil.

"Remember? The blood was covering his face," said Chris.

Benno was glad Chris remembered, because he'd forgotten.

"Yeah, but what about the rest of him? Wouldn't he still look different?"

"Dirk probably alternated his appearance to look like Jordan," said Kirsten, unaware of her malapropism, "so, without the face, no one could tell them apart—except Lady Violetta, who noticed the fingers."

The rest of the children all looked at their fingers curiously, silently comparing others' to their own.

Benno was frantically trying to come up with a way to end the Q and A. In the end he was saved when Brenda walked in with a stack of—

"MOVIES!!!" There was a blur of movement, the sound of a stampede, and all at once Benno was alone.

Neil stuck his head back in long enough to say, "Thanks for the story!"

"You're welcome." Benno leaned back and sighed a long sigh. *Now* he was alone.

Almost. "You told it wrong," a voice grumbled. Myrna got up and headed for the door. "The cook should've been the murderer," she said, exiting.

After a moment, Benno chuckled to himself. "Well, I liked it," he said quietly.

Epilogue

The darkened hospital room made Violet uneasy. She tapped on the door uncertainly. "Mr. Mayor? Mr. Pressler?"

There was no answer from the figure in the bed.

She cleared her throat. "I was told you wanted to see me. A-are you awake?" She stepped closer. She was surprised at how small Pressler looked, not at all the dashing figure he always cut in his public appearances.

The man's eyes fluttered open and focused on her.

She wasn't quite sure what to say. "I'm...glad you're okay," she managed lamely.

"You saved me." Pressler's voice was gratingly hoarse.

"Well, Chuck was the one who—"

Pressler shook his head slowly, emphatically. He jabbed a finger at her. "You!" His hand wobbled, likely a result of the drugs he was on, treating him for hypothermia.

"I should let you get some rest—"

With a groggy gesture, he motioned for her to come closer. She hesitated, then obeyed, drawing up to his bedside.

"You saved me," Pressler repeated.

Finally Violet nodded. "Yes," she said, "I did."

He cleared his throat. "I bet you think I'm a petty, ungrateful, unscrupulous bastard." He looked into her eyes. "If that's what you're thinking..."

With lightning speed, he seized her by the collar. *"Then you're damn right!"*

Violet fought back, but his grip was iron-tight.

Through his teeth Pressler rasped, "If you think that saving me changes anything, if you think I'd have any second thoughts about getting even with you for interfering in my business... *think again!!"*

He lapsed into a severe fit of coughing, and let her go. She stumbled against the wall, shaken. Her instinct for flight was screaming at her to get as far away from the man as she could, but she swallowed her panic and stood her ground, waiting until Pressler stopped coughing and sank back onto his bed, exhausted.

She took a tremulous step toward him. His capacity for speech apparently spent, he gave her the most threatening scowl he could muster.

In a quavering voice, Violet said, "You know that recording?"

Pressler's eyes widened ever so slightly.

"The recording of Rob Mulroy's meeting with Tuck Fleagle just before Rob was shot—remember that?"

Pressler held his breath.

"Fleagle said I was meant to come here and fight a great evil. Some people in town think he meant the serial killer. Wouldn't it be funny, though...if it was you?"

With that, she left.

* * *

Jen had had barely more than a bite to eat for dinner, and Violet and Cy had both lost their appetites, so all three of them were relieved when they arrived home to find that the Dosleys had prepared a veritable feast. With the generator up and running, the house was warm and welcoming.

Blinking sleepy eyes at the head of the dining table, Jen reached out and took Cy's and Violet's hands in each of hers. "I'm really proud of you two," she said. "I know it's corny, but pulling together and helping out is what makes this a community."

"Do you need us to help out again tomorrow?" asked Violet.

Jen groaned and winced. "Ask me in the morning." Giving Cy's hand a small shake, she added, "And then you can tell me who that boy was."

Cy rolled her eyes. Violet gave her a brightly curious look. "It's not what you think," Cy told her.

Violet didn't bring it up again until after dinner. "At least tell me who hit on whom," she whispered to Cy.

"I hit him—with a door."

Before Violet could puzzle that out, Kristy approached them and said, "I just got Rosie to sleep. My moms and I were wondering if you want to join us for..." She held up a shiny object.

"Oh!" Cy looked at a nearby calendar hanging on the wall. "Yeah, of course! Let's do it over here."

A few minutes later saw Jen, Cy, Violet, Joy, Fran, and Kristy gathered in front of the fireplace, their faces aglow from the long match held by Fran. As she lit the candles of the menorah sitting on the mantle, Cy and Jen read aloud from a piece of paper, but Violet discovered—to her surprise—that she already knew the words. The six of them spoke as one:

"Baruch atah adonai, eloheinu melech ha'olam, asher kid'shanu b'mitzvotav v'tsivanu l'hadlik ner shel Hanukkah. A-a-men."

WINTER IN VEIL

A Mystery Novella Series
by Miles Ledoux

#1 VIOLET
#2 GOOD WITCH, BAD WITCH
#3 JOHNSON'S WELDER
#4 RING AROUND THE ROSIE
#5 POP GOES THE WEASEL
#6 APRIL
#7 OVERKILL
#8 THE THIRD WILL
#9 SALT & VINEGAR
#10 MEMORY LANE
#11 THE IMPOSTOR
#12 KISS ME QUICK
#13 BEHIND THE DARKNESS

Next time in Veil...

Violet eyed the terrain critically. Of the few gaps between the trees that allowed for easy passage, none contained ground that would make walking easy. She tried one experimentally and nearly twisted her ankle. No, she couldn't imagine anyone hiking farther into the woods than this, not without a proper trail. If Roberta really had made it this far—for whatever reason—then, unless she had a specific route planned out, her next act would've been to turn around and head back home. So why hadn't she reappeared?

Violet turned around and began to head back.

An arm closed tightly round her throat and suffocated her.

About the Author

Miles Ledoux was born in upstate New York and started writing murder mysteries at the age of nine. His first paid writing gig was in 2007, when a local theatre chose one of his plays for their summer melodrama. He received other royalties after moving to Los Angeles for graduate school, where he wrote, directed, and produced several mystery dessert theatre plays. He also started a side business designing and running mystery party games while working as a martial arts instructor.

Currently the author resides in Springfield, Vermont. Despite having lived in five different states, he has remained active in community theatre as a playwright, director, and actor. He also has a YouTube channel where he compares Agatha Christie adaptations to the books they were based on. His handle is @MysteryMiles.

Miles loves books, cats, music, Star Trek, Peanuts, and owns an ever-growing number of variations of the board game Clue. His favorite author is Lloyd Alexander.

You can connect with me on:

https://www.ledouxmysteries.com

www.ingramcontent.com/pod-product-compliance
Lightning Source LLC
Chambersburg PA
CBHW072233190626
46809CB00017B/1900

9781882508877